P9-ECS-862

3 1111 01179 7865

Calhoun, M.   E   74989
Wobble the witch cat.

DATE DUE

DATE DUE	
DEC 1 0 2003	
APR 1 3 2004	
AUG 0 5 2004	
OCT 2 0 2004	
DEC 0 7 2004	
JAN 0 3 2005	
MAR 1 2 2005	
OCT 1 9 2005	
NOV 0 9 2005	
APR 2 6 2006	
AUG 1 5 2006	
OCT 1 7 2006	

DISCARD

GAYLORD   PRINTED IN U.S.A.

WOBBLE, THE WITCH CAT

© 1958 by Mary Calhoun. All rights reserved. Published simultaneously in the Dominion of Canada by George J. McLeod Limited, Toronto. Printed in the United States of America. Library of Congress Catalog Card No. 58-5018.

WITCH CAT

CAT

by

MARY CALHOUN

pictures by

ROGER DUVOISIN

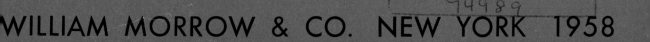

WILLIAM MORROW & CO. NEW YORK 1958

Once upon a Halloween
there was a good witch named Maggie
who owned
a very grumpy witch cat named Wobble.
They lived together
in a teetery little house
on the edge of town.

Maggie was a fat, chuckling old lady
with short, gray hair.
Wobble was as cross as he was black.

He hadn't always been cross.
Once he had been just as good as Maggie.
It was all the fault of a new broomstick
that Maggie had gotten
for the last Halloween.
It had a thin, slippery handle
and it was so hard to ride on
that Wobble was afraid he would fall off.
He had even tried
wrapping his tail around the stick.
But he just couldn't balance
on the thin seat.

Just as the broomstick
rose from the ground, he *did* fall off.
He climbed on again quickly,
but it gave him a bad scare.

What's worse, all the other witch cats
had laughed at Wobble,
as he wobbled across the sky.
Now it was almost Halloween again,
and Wobble grew very cross
as he worried about riding the broomstick.
He grumped.
And he yowled.
And he ran under Maggie's feet,
just on purpose.

Only yesterday
he had almost upset the old lady,
as she carried her pans of witch's brew
to the oven.

She was making magic wish cookies
to set out for the children
when they came trick-or-treating.
Wobble refused to go out
and howl on fences,
as a proper witch cat should.
Instead, he crouched in a corner,
twitching his whiskers
and grumbling to himself
about the broomstick.
The day before Halloween
he even knocked the jack-o'-lantern
out of the window.
That evening Maggie said gaily,
"Tomorrow night we ride again!"
And Wobble, that unhappy cat,
actually humped his back and spat at her.
Spat at his old friend, Maggie!

Late that night, while Maggie slept,
Wobble went tip-tip-tip
on his soft black feet to the broom closet.
There hung the witch's broomstick,
shining faintly with magic,
all ready for Halloween.
Wobble grabbed the stick with his teeth
and pulled it down.
Out the back door he pulled it,

out through the back yard,
out to the trash barrel.
He pushed the broom into the barrel.
And then he scampered back to the house
for a good night's sleep.

Early the next morning
the rubbish truck came along
and took the witch's broomstick away.
All that day
Wobble was in a much better temper.
When the sky began to darken,
and Maggie got out her black cape
and pointed black hat,
Wobble just licked his fur and purred.
"Time to dust off my broomstick
and get ready to go," Maggie told him.
"We must sweep the stars clean
in our part of the sky
so the children here will be able to see
when they go trick-or-treating."
Wobble just grinned a black witch-cat grin.

Maggie went to the broom closet
and opened the door.
The broomstick was gone!

There was only a great empty place
where the broom usually hung.
"Oh, fiddle!
Now where did I put that broom?"
Maggie worried.
"I keep it hanging
in this closet all year."
She looked on the back porch.
No broomstick!
The witch cat chased his tail.

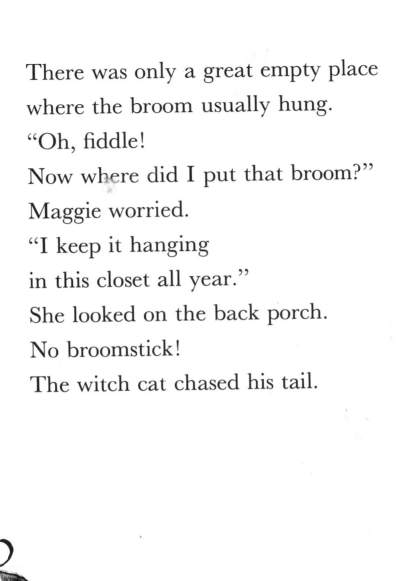

Maggie scurried all over the house,
peering into every nook and cranny.
But no broomstick anywhere!
Wobble danced on his hind legs,
pretending he was chasing a fly.
"Oh dear, where is my magic broomstick?"
the old witch cried.

"We can't fly up into the sky without it.
And there's no time
to go to the witch of the mountain
for a new one."
Wobble sat down and tried to look sad.
But his yellow eyes gleamed.
"It's almost dark now," Maggie muttered,
pulling at her hair.

"Whatever shall we do? I wonder if I have
an extra broom in the closet?"
She opened the closet door again.
No, there was nothing in the closet
but her vacuum cleaner.
Maggie started to turn away;
then she looked back at the vacuum cleaner.
What was that strange glow about it?

"Galloping ghosts!" she shouted.
"It looks magic!"
All year the broom had been hanging
over the vacuum cleaner in the closet.
"Maybe the magic of the broom
dripped off onto the vacuum cleaner!"
Maggie cried.
"Maybe the cleaner will fly!"

Wobble stopped waving his long tail
and began to look worried.
"We'll just have to try it,"
the old witch said.

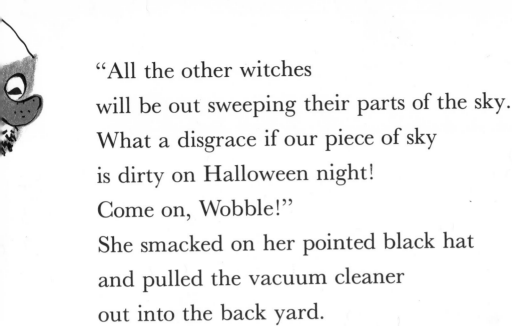

"All the other witches
will be out sweeping their parts of the sky.
What a disgrace if our piece of sky
is dirty on Halloween night!
Come on, Wobble!"
She smacked on her pointed black hat
and pulled the vacuum cleaner
out into the back yard.
But Wobble ran under the stove.
He crouched there, yowling with fear.

Maggie got down on her knees
and tried to pull him out.
"Nice Wobble! Don't be afraid!"
She tried to soothe him.
The cat just braced his feet and growled.
At last Maggie had to drag him out.
She tucked him tightly under her arm
and went back to the vacuum cleaner.
The machine glowed strangely
in the moonlight.
"Now, I'll ride on the handle,
and you can ride on the bag in back,"
she told Wobble.
"And don't you dare jump off!"

Wobble sat down stiffly and dug his claws
into the cloth of the bag.
He hoped the vacuum cleaner wouldn't fly.
"Abracadabra, sis-boom-baaa!"
Maggie shouted.
The vacuum cleaner trembled,
gave a jerk,
and up into the air it rose!
High into the Halloween sky
sailed Maggie and Wobble
on the magic vacuum cleaner.
Suddenly
Wobble realized something wonderful.
The vacuum cleaner's bag
made a nice wide seat.
He wasn't wobbling!

"Meow!" he cried happily.
Then he curled up on the bag
and began to lick his fur.
Wobble was going to enjoy
this Halloween ride!
As Maggie and Wobble
flew near a flock of witches.

all the cats screeched with laughter.
"Here comes wobbling Wobble!"
And then they stared in surprise.
For Wobble
flipped his tail smartly at them,
and sailed on by,
comfortable as on his own cushion at home.

When the boys and girls
came out of their houses,
dressed as clowns and cowboys
and witches and ghosts,
they looked up at the sky.
"Oh! Oh!" cried a little girl
in a Red Ridinghood cape.
"I think I saw a witch up there!
But what's she riding on?"

The other children looked up and,
sure enough,
flying across the moon was a little speck.

It looked like a witch and a cat
doing loop-the-loops on a vacuum cleaner.